Beetle Boddiker

Priscilla Cummings

illustrated by
Marcy Dunn Ramsey

Tidewater Publishers
Centreville, MD 21617

Beneath the back steps, by a rock in the shade,
Beetle Boddiker lives in the house that he made.
A jumble of sticks and a tumble of leaves,
it's a simple bug house. *But don't step on it, please!*

You have to look close. He's not easy to see.

He's a shiny, dark beetle and small as a pea.

His hat is a derby. He wears a bow tie.

And he likes to say, "Gee! Fiddledee. Me, oh, my!"

A cautious old beetle,
    he rarely leaves home.
"The backyard is a jungle," he says.
    "I won't roam!"

But then in the mail came a nice invitation.
His brother Nevins wrote:
    "Come to a huge celebration!
    A birthday cake! Fruit juice!
    Some games! And much more!"
Although Nevins left out
    who this party was for.

"I can't," Boddiker thought. Nevins lived far away,
in a rusty tin can, in a dark alleyway.
A long trip indeed for a beetle's six feet.
It meant crossing the yard—and then crossing the street!

"Oh, gee, fiddledee," Beetle Boddiker said.
"Me, oh, my," he groaned loudly
    and shook his small head.
But then he recalled his baby bug days,
how he learned from his brother
    such good beetle ways.
Nevins taught him to hide.
    Nevins taught him to scurry.

"Watch *me*," Nevins said, "and you won't have to worry!"
Beetle Boddiker knew that for Nevins he'd go.
He missed his big brother a lot. And so . . .

He set out the next day on grass wet with dew,
and went slipping and sliding in boots that were new.
He climbed up one blade, then he slid down another,
at the start of his journey to see Nevins, his brother.
While sliding he fell on a soft bed of clover,
but he got up again and started all over.

He made way for spiders and grasshoppers too.
He was never quite sure of just what they might do.

When ladybugs passed, he became rather shy.
He would tip his black hat as they scooted on by.

Early on in the trip he discovered a hose,
climbed aboard and then said, "Wonder where this hose goes."
He zipped right along the new slick rubber road
until—*oops*—he was stopped by a GREAT BIG FAT TOAD!

The toad croaked out, "Ribbit!"
Beetle Boddiker sneezed.

Then he slid off the hose and fell—*smack*—on two bees!
The bees were not pleased so Boddiker moved on.
Thereafter arriving at the edge of the lawn.

The driveway was next. A big ocean of rocks.
Beetle Boddiker wished he had worn extra socks.
He climbed and he climbed. When he reached the last hill
some dark clouds filled the sky and the breeze brought a chill.

He knew right away this was no place to stay.

But as soon as he ran, a storm swept him away!

Down the gutter he went on a river of rain!

Down the street he went—*help!*—then—*oh, no!*

So cold and so dark, but he spotted a leaf.

As he pulled himself on, he sighed with relief.

"What now?" he cried softly and wrung out his hat.

"It was not in my plans to be detoured like that!"

"Oh, gee. Fiddledee." He peered up at the sky.
"I just have to get out. I can't sit here and cry."
So slowly, so *s-l-o-w-l-y,* he started to crawl.
Inch by inch, brick by brick, up the towering wall.

He made it at last, but his derby hat drooped.
He was tired and wet and his thin shoulders stooped.
"Oh, Nevins," he moaned. "Will I ever be there?"
Beetle Boddiker longed to sit down in a chair.

By then it was dusk.
Fast approaching was night.
But at last—Nevins's can.
It was there! In his sight!
A lightening bug flashed and
    its light lit the way.
Beetle Boddiker heard
    someone whisper and say:

"Gee whiz! Here he is! Hide the cake! Now get ready!"

Someone else said, "The camera! Quick! Hold it steady!"

His brother yelled, "Hey, there! What took you so long?"

As a whole crowd jumped out, cheered, and burst into song:

"Happy Birthday, Beetle Boddiker! Happy Birthday to you!"

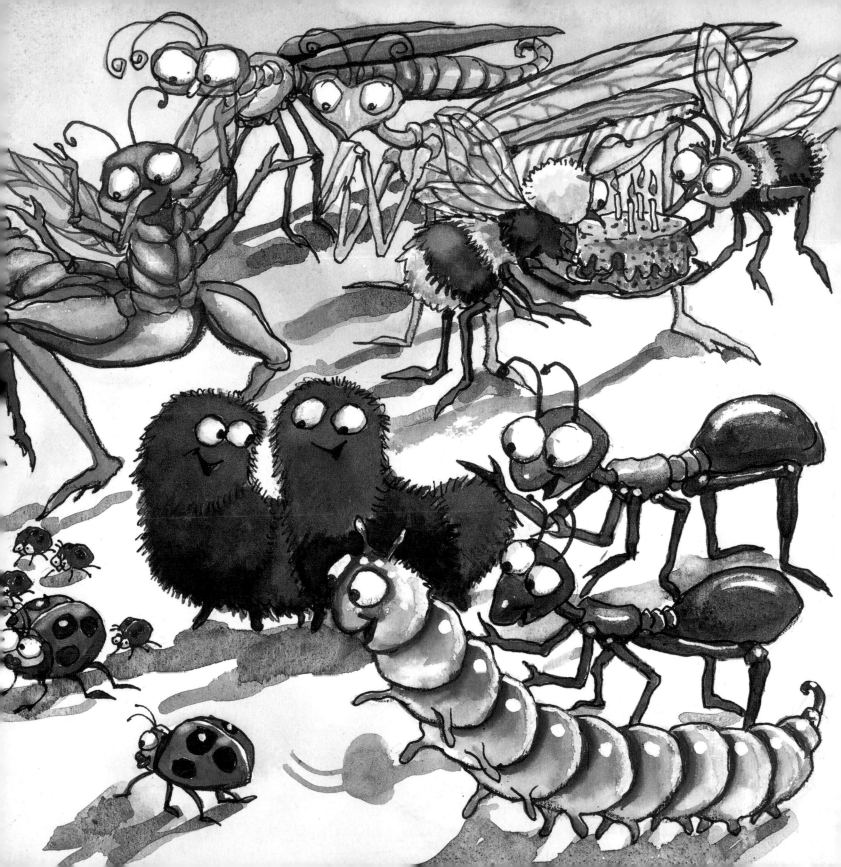

"Oh, gee! Fiddledee! What's that you just said?"
Beetle Boddiker grinned as he scratched his wet head.
"Surprise!" Nevins told him. "This party's for you—
a surprise birthday party. The best we could do!"

Confetti was flying. It covered a slug.

Beetle Boddiker blushed. He gave Nevins a hug.

"I'm so glad we're brothers and that we're together,"
Beetle Boddiker said. "I will love you forever!"

A moth fluttered by and passed out thick slices
of sweet cake that she'd made
from some seeds and some spices.
Beetle Boddiker thanked her, but just couldn't eat.
He said, "Let me sit down first and rest my poor feet."
When somebody asked him how come he was wet,

Beetle Boddiker joked, "'Twas a trip to forget!
I practically drowned!" he cried. "Yes! But all the same,
I assure everyone that I'm quite glad I came.
Just one thing I ask." A smile lit up his face.
"The next party we have? It will be at *my place*!"